COLLECTION
— OF —
STORYTIME
FAVORITES

T 13236

HarperCollins*Publishers*

COLLECTION — OF — STORYTIME FAVORITES

HarperCollins*Publishers*

ISBN-10: 0-06-169156-9
ISBN-13: 978-0-06-169156-0

An I Can Read Book®

The Big Balloon Race

story by Eleanor Coerr
pictures by Carolyn Croll

HarperCollins*Publishers*

For Julian, balloon detective
—E.C.

For Joshua and Anna
—C.C.

~ 1 ~

Balloons, Balloons!

It was the day

of the big balloon race.

Ariel got up early

and hurried to her mother's room.

"Please," she asked, "can I go up

in the balloon with you?"

5

Carlotta the Great

was putting on her blue dress

with the fancy gold braid.

"You are too young," she said,

"and winning a race

is hard work."

"But I can help," said Ariel.

Carlotta smiled.

"You can help by riding

in the buggy with your father

to the finish line."

"Oh, thumps!" said Ariel.

Sadly, she went outside.

7

Balloon Farm was a strange farm.

In the yard

half-filled balloons sat

like giant mushrooms.

People came from all over

to buy balloons

made by Mr. Myers.

Ariel watched her father

fold Carlotta's balloon, *Lucky Star.*

"I wish I could be an aeronaut

like Mama," she said.

"When you are older,"

said Mr. Myers.

10

"Now it is time to go."

Carlotta, Ariel, and Mr. Myers

climbed into the buggy.

Lucky Star followed in a wagon.

There was a great whoop-de-doo

at the fairgrounds.

Thousands of people were there

to see the balloon race.

It was a big event in 1882.

OOMPAH! OOMPAH! OOMPAH!

played the band.

Two balloons were already

in the air.

They were tied to the ground

by long ropes.

Acrobats swung from one basket

to the other.

Lucky Star and its net

were spread out on the ground.

PFFFTTTTTT!

Lighter-than-air hydrogen gas

hissed into the balloon.

It slowly grew

until it was taller

than the house

on Balloon Farm.

Twelve strong men

held *Lucky Star* down.

Nearby, another balloon

grew fat and tall.

It was *Flying Cloud,*

a ball of bright colors.

Its captain, Bernard the Brave,

was the best gentleman aeronaut

in America.

Carlotta the Great

was the best lady aeronaut.

It would be a close race.

SCIENCE AND ARTS ACADEMY

"I bet you will win,"

Ariel told her mother.

Carlotta gave her a kiss.

"You can sit in the basket

until it is time to go."

Ariel got inside the basket

18

and talked to Harry the pigeon.

Harry went on every flight.

Sometimes he took messages

from Carlotta to Balloon Farm.

The mayor began a long speech.

He talked on and on.

19

So Ariel climbed inside

the Odds and Ends box.

It was quieter there,

and cozy and warm.

Soon she was fast asleep.

Ariel did not hear

the mayor's last words.

"There is a south wind," he said,

"so the finish line will be

the other side

of Devil's Punchbowl Lake."

Ariel did not even hear the drums.

TARUUUUUM!

The aeronauts

stepped into their baskets.

The crowd cheered.

Mr. Myers waved to Carlotta.

"Good luck!"

She waved her nobby sailor hat.

"Hands off!" Carlotta ordered.

The men let go of the ropes.

With a jolt,

Lucky Star took off.

~ 2 ~
Ups and Downs

Ariel woke up.

"What happened?" she asked.

Carlotta stared.

"Ariel! What have you done?"

she cried.

"We are aloft!"

Ariel looked over the side.

Sure enough,

they were off the ground.

Below, someone yelled, "Stop!

There is a stowaway in that basket!"

Mr. Myers waved his arms

and shouted something.

Ariel waved back.

"Oooo!" she cried.

"It's like being a bird."

She watched the crowd

set out for the finish line.

Some were in buggies,

some were in wagons,

and others were on fast horses.

A crosswind tugged at the balloon.

WHOOOOSH!

Lucky Star swooped away over a farm.

Dogs barked

and ran around in circles.

Pigs squealed.

Chickens squawked.

A horse reared and galloped away.

SCRUUUUNCH!

Lucky Star's basket

scraped the treetops.

"Can we go higher?" asked Ariel.

"The balloon and ballast
are for only one passenger,"
said Carlotta.

"You are extra weight."

She dropped one bag of sand

over the side.

Up went *Lucky Star*.

The farm got smaller and smaller.

It looked like a toy.

Then it was gone.

"Dear me!" said Carlotta.

"An updraft is sucking us
into that raincloud."

She pulled on the blue valve rope
to let out some gas.

Lucky Star did not fall.

Ariel stared up into netting
that looked like a spiderweb.

"Why don't you pull
the red rope, too?" she asked.

"That is the rip cord,"
said her mother. "It lets
the gas out all at once."

Carlotta tied her hat snugly

under her chin.

"Sit down!" she ordered.

"And hang on!"

Ariel hugged

her mother's sturdy legs

in their fancy blue gaiters.

Lucky Star was in the middle

of a misty, wet, bumpy cloud.

The basket went back and forth,

up and down,

then around and around.

"I feel sick," said Ariel.

"A good aeronaut keeps calm,"

said Carlotta.

"The balloon will cool

and we will go down."

She was right.

36

In a few minutes *Lucky Star*

was sailing away from the cloud.

Carlotta checked everything.

"Ropes and toggles

are in fine trim,"

she said.

She read the altimeter

that hung around her neck.

"We are about 2000 feet up."

She studied the map and compass.

"We are heading south."

"Look!" said Ariel.

"The lake is straight ahead."

Just then they saw *Flying Cloud*.

"He is beating us," said Ariel.

"He will win the gold medal."

Carlotta shook her head.

"I have a few tricks yet," she said.

"Perhaps we can find

a faster stream of air below us."

41

She valved out gas.

Down...down...down

went *Lucky Star*.

It was sinking too fast—

and toward a town!

Carlotta tossed handfuls

of sand over the side.

Lucky Star moved up

and skimmed the rooftops.

People stopped whatever

they were doing and stared

at the balloon.

Suddenly wind stung Ariel's cheeks.

"Heigh-ho!" cried Carlotta.

"We found the airstream!"

It was Ariel who first saw

a spiky church steeple

coming toward them.

"Look out!" she yelled.

She closed her eyes and hung on.

Carlotta threw out more sand.

Just in time!

Lucky Star soared over the steeple.

Now *Flying Cloud* was behind.

"If we don't hit another updraft,"

said Carlotta,

"we might win."

Soon they were sweeping

over the lake.

"There is only a little sand left,"

Carlotta said.

"Let's hope the wind

blows us right across."

The air was cold.

Lucky Star's gas cooled.

They went down.

Carlotta tossed out

the last handful of sand.

But it was not enough.

"Oh, thumps!" cried Ariel.

"We'll crash into the lake!"

"Let's keep our wits about us,"

said Carlotta,

"and make the basket lighter."

Ariel helped throw out

a raincoat, rubber boots,

the Odds and Ends box,

and the anchor.

Everything went over the side

except Harry and his cage.

49

~ 3 ~
Ariel to the Rescue

Lucky Star wobbled

and took a giant step.

"Lean on this side," said Carlotta.

The basket creaked

and tilted toward shore.

Lucky Star was almost there, when

SPLAAAAASH!

The basket plunked into the water.

But it didn't sink.

The balloon kept it afloat.

"We lost the race," cried Ariel,

"and it is all my fault.

I am extra weight."

Ariel knew what she had to do.

She held her nose

and jumped into the lake.

The water was only up to her waist.

"Good gracious!"

said her mother.

"That was brave,

but it will not help.

Even without you,

the basket is too wet and heavy

to go up again."

Just then *Flying Cloud*

began to come down.

"Our last chance!" cried Carlotta.

She threw the guide rope to Ariel.

"Pull!

Pull us to shore!

Hurry!"

Ariel grabbed the rope

and waded onto the beach.

Lucky Star was easy to pull

with a balloon holding it up.

"Splendid!" cried Carlotta.

She jumped out and dragged

the basket to higher ground.

A minute later

Flying Cloud landed.

"We won! We won!"

shouted Ariel and Carlotta.

They were laughing and hugging

and crying all at the same time.

Bernard the Brave

anchored his balloon to a tree.

Then he came over

and shook Carlotta's hand.

"Congratulations!" he said.

"I see that *Lucky Star* has a crew."

He wrapped Ariel in a blanket.

"Thank you, sir," said Ariel.

Bernard smiled.

"Why, it is my pleasure."

Carlotta sent Harry home

with a victory message

to Balloon Farm.

Soon the crowd arrived.

Mr. Myers rode up in the buggy.

Carlotta told him

how Ariel had helped win the race.

"Ariel," he said,

"I'm proud of you."

The mayor gave Ariel

the gold medal.

Carlotta hugged Ariel.

"I'm proud of you, too," she said.

"Perhaps you *are* old enough to fly."

Ariel smiled happily.

She was sure of it.

The Golly Sisters Go West

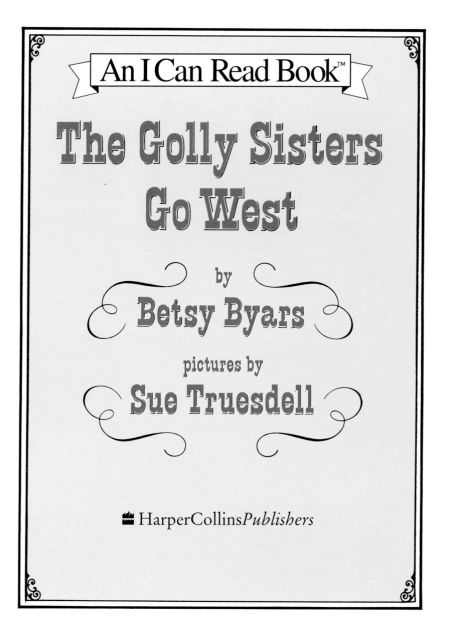

An I Can Read Book™

The Golly Sisters Go West

by

Betsy Byars

pictures by

Sue Truesdell

HarperCollins*Publishers*

For Paul and Scott

The Golly Sisters Go West

The Golly sisters sat in their wagon.

They were going west.

"Go," May-May said to the horse.

The horse did not go.

"This makes me mad," May-May said.

"Our wagon is ready.

Our songs and dances are ready.

And the horse will not go."

"It makes me mad too," said Rose.

"Something is wrong with this horse."

Rose got down from the wagon.

May-May got down too.

They walked around the horse.

"Do you see anything wrong?"

May-May asked.

"No, but something is wrong,"
said Rose.
"When we say, 'Go,'
the horse does not go."
"And if the horse does not go,
we do not go," said May-May.

Suddenly, Rose said,

"Sister!

I just remembered something.

There is a horse word for 'go.'"

"A horse word?" said May-May.

"What is it?"

"Giddy-up!" Rose said.

The horse went.

"Stop! Stop!" cried May-May.

"Is there a horse word for stop?"

"Whoa," said Rose.

"WHOA!" cried May-May.

The horse stopped.

The sisters got into the wagon.

Rose took the reins.

"Giddy-up, horse," she said.

The horse went.

May-May said,

"Now that we know the right words,

we can go west."

"Yes," said Rose.

"We are on our way!"

The Golly Sisters Give a Show

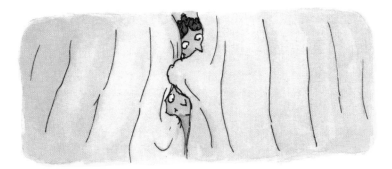

It was the Golly sisters' first show.

They peeped around the curtain.

Men and women were there.

Children were there.

Even dogs were there.

"Oh, am I ready!" said May-May.

"You open the curtain,

and I will go first."

18

"I want to go first," said Rose.

"You got to wear the blue dress,

so I get to go first," said May-May.

20

"I got to wear the blue dress

because you look funny in blue,"

said Rose.

"Who says I look funny in blue?"

asked May-May.

"Everybody!" said Rose.

"Give me the name of one person

who says I look funny in blue."

"Everybody!" said Rose.

"I knew it," said May-May.

"You cannot think of one person."

"I can."

"Cannot!"

"Can!"

"Then who?"

"Hmmmm, let me think," said Rose.

"See! There is not one person.

Admit it! Admit it! Admit it!"

cried May-May.

"All right, I admit it," said Rose.

"We will both go first.

We will sing and dance together."

Rose pulled the curtain.

"Oh, dear," May-May said,

"everyone got tired and went home.

Are you going to cry, Rose?"

"No," said Rose.

"Everyone did not go home.

The dogs are still here."

"Sister, do we give shows for dogs?"

"I do," said Rose.

"Then I do too," said May-May.

So May-May and Rose

gave a show for the dogs.

"This is wonderful!" May-May said.

"It sure is," sang Rose.

The Golly Sisters Get Lost

"We are lost," May-May said.

"I was afraid of that," said Rose.

"Are you worried, May-May?"

"No. I know what to do

when I am lost."

"You do? What?" asked Rose.

"First," said May-May,

"get in the back of the wagon.

Second,

make a cup of tea.

Third—"

"Wait, May-May, let me stop the horse.

I cannot make tea when he is moving."

"No!" said May-May.

"Do *not* stop the horse.

That is the *third* thing."

"Is there a fourth thing?" asked Rose.

"Yes!" said May-May. "Sing!

You start, Rose."

"Okay,"

said Rose.

"I will sing

'The Lost Gollys.'

It is about us."

Rose sang.

"Now it is my turn,"

said May-May.

"I will sing

'The Brave Gollys.'

It is about us too."

30

While May-May sang,

the wagon kept moving.

Then Rose sang again,

then May-May sang.

Then they sang together.

"I wonder if we are still lost?"
asked May-May.

"I will check," said Rose.

Just then they heard clapping.

They looked out of the wagon.

They were in the middle of a town.

Men and women were there.

Children and dogs were there.

34

"We gave a show!" May-May said.

"A wonderful show!" said Rose.

"We should get lost more often!"

35

The Golly sisters bowed.

"Thank you, thank you," they said.

The Horse Gives a Show

"I want the horse to dance

in the show," said May-May.

"No, May-May," said Rose,

"the horse cannot dance."

"Give him a chance, Rose.

Remember when we started?

No one thought *we* could dance.

No one thought we could sing."

"May-May, the horse cannot dance!"

38

"Trust me, Rose. You say—

Here is my sister, May-May,

and her dancing horse, and

the horse and I will do the rest."

That night May-May got on the horse.

"We are ready," she called.

Rose said to the people,

"Here is my sister, May-May,

and her dancing horse."

"Let's go, horse,"
May-May said.

The horse
did not move.

"Here is my sister,
May-May,
and her dancing horse,"
Rose said again.

"Come on, horse,"
said May-May.

The horse did not move.

Rose said, "While we are waiting

for May-May and her dancing horse,

I will sing a song."

When May-May heard that,

she said, "Giddy-up!"

The horse moved!

He jumped onto the stage.

He jumped off the stage.

May-May screamed, *"Eeeeeeeeee!"*

43

The horse ran through the town.

The horse ran out of the town.

"Well, that is too bad," Rose said.

"There will be no dancing horse.

No May-May either.

But do not worry.

I will do her songs and dances."

Late that night, May-May came back.

She fell onto her bed.

"Sister, you were right," she said.

"The horse cannot dance."

May-May Loses Her Hat

"May-May, are you ready?" asked Rose.

"No, I am not!" said May-May.

"My song is 'In My Pretty Red Hat,'

and I cannot find my red hat!"

"Want me to go first?" asked Rose.

"All right, but this makes me mad.

It was *my* turn to go first."

While Rose was singing,

May-May looked for her hat.

When Rose came off the stage,

May-May was still looking

for her hat.

"I want my hat!" she yelled.

"Did you
look under
my bed?"
asked Rose.

"Why would my hat

be under your bed?"

May-May asked.

She looked under Rose's bed.

There was the hat!

"Now I am really mad," said May-May.

"You *hid* my hat!"

"No harm has been done, May-May.

You can sing now," said Rose.

"I wanted to sing first!

First! First! First!"

yelled May-May.

52

"Stop!" cried Rose.

"You are squashing my hair.

May-May! Stop!"

May-May stopped

and looked at her hat.

"Rose!" she said.

"First I could not sing

because I could not find my hat.

Now I cannot sing

because I squashed my hat."

"My hair, too," said Rose.

"Rose," said May-May,

"tell the people

I will do a sad dance,

'The Dance of the Squashed Hat.'"

"People," said Rose, "here is May-May

and 'The Dance of the Squashed Hat.'"

May-May danced.

The people began to clap.

May-May turned to her sister.

"I forgive you, Rose," she said.

"I forgive you too," said Rose.

The Golly Sisters Are Scared

It was a dark night.

There was no moon.

"I hear something," May-May said.

"Something is outside our wagon."

"What will we do?" asked Rose.

"One of us will have to go outside,"

said May-May.

"I heard the noise, so you go."

"Why should *I* go?

It's your noise," said Rose.

"Do I have to do everything?"

asked May-May.

"I am not going to go," said Rose.

"Then I'm not going to go either,"

said May-May. "Nyah!"

"Nyah yourself!" said Rose.

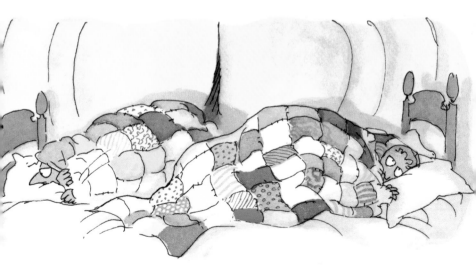

May-May sat up.

"Remember our first show, Rose?
Remember how we fussed because
you said I look funny in blue?"

"Yes, I remember," said Rose.

"I remember we fussed so long
that everyone went home."

"Maybe we have done it again,"
May-May said.

"I do not hear anything now, do you?"

"I do not hear a thing," said Rose.

May-May said, "Rose,

we must never fuss again,

unless…"

61

"Unless we hear something
outside our wagon," Rose said.
"Rose,
that is what *I* was going to say.
You did not let me finish!
Why did you say—"
"May-May?"
"What?"
"Good night."
"Good night, Rose."

And the moon came out.

And the stars shone.

And the Golly sisters fell asleep.

An I Can Read Book®

The Outside Dog

story by Charlotte Pomerantz
pictures by Jennifer Plecas

HarperCollins*Publishers*

For Flora Cass Gosch

—C. P.

Contents

Spanish words in the story:

Doña	*(DON-ya)*	Madame
Colmado	*(col-MA-doe)*	Grocery store
Vete	*(VEH-tay)*	Scram
Abuelito	*(ab-wel-EE-toe)*	Grandpa
Qué raro	*(kay RA-ro)*	How strange
¿Entiendes?	*(en-TYEN-days)*	Understand?
Qué cosa	*(kay KO-sa)*	My goodness
Lo vi	*(lo VEE)*	I saw him
¿Qué pasa?	*(kay PA-sa)*	What's the matter?

Marisol Wants a Dog

Marisol lived with her grandfather
in Puerto Rico.
Their home was in a little village
on the side of a hill.
There was a big mango tree
in the yard,
and mountains all around.
Below, was the warm blue sea.

Their neighbor up the hill

was Doña Elvira.

She owned a little *colmado*,

where they bought their groceries.

6

Their neighbor down the hill
was a fisherman named Nando.
Sometimes, in the early morning,
Marisol went fishing with him.

There were many dogs on the hill.

They were strays.

No one owned or took care of them.

Marisol had always wanted a dog,

but Grandfather said they had fleas

and ticks and who knows what.

Whenever a dog came into the yard,

Grandfather chased it away.

"*¡Vete!*" he yelled. "Scram!"

9

One day, Grandfather and Marisol
came home and found a dog
sitting near their house.
He was a skinny brown mutt
with perky ears and big brown eyes.

10

Grandfather chased him away.

But that evening, the dog came back.

When Marisol thought

her grandfather was not looking,

she sneaked out and petted him.

"Marisol," said Grandfather,

"I told you not to pet the dogs.

They have fleas and ticks

and who knows what."

"But, *Abuelito*, this one does not,"

said Marisol. "Look!"

"*¡Qué raro!*" Grandfather said.

"There is not a flea on him."

"So may I pet him?" asked Marisol.

"You may pet this one.

But only this one.

And don't feed him a thing!

¿Entiendes?" said Grandfather.

"Once you feed a stray dog,

he never goes away."

13

Later, when they were eating

pork chops and potatoes,

the dog came and sat very quietly

outside the screen door.

"Grandpa, do you think he is hungry?"

asked Marisol.

"Of course he is hungry.

Every stray dog on this hill

is hungry," said Grandfather.

"If I worried about that,

I would be feeding twenty dogs."

15

Grandfather piled the leftover bones

onto a plate.

"What are you going to do

with the bones?" asked Marisol.

"Throw them in the garbage,

of course," said Grandfather.

"Why don't you give them to the dog?"

asked Marisol.

Grandfather sighed. "All right.

Just this once. But not here.

Out on the road, away from the house.

I don't want him to think

that this is his home."

They walked to the road.

The dog followed.

When Grandfather dumped

the plate of bones,

three other dogs came running.

"Scram!" Grandfather shouted.

"Let this one eat. *¡Vete!*"

A Collar for Pancho

Grandfather sipped dark coffee
in the doorway.

Marisol patted the dog.

"He is sort of nice looking
for a mutt, isn't he, Grandpa?"

"He's okay," said Grandfather.

19

"I don't think he is all mutt,"

said Marisol.

"Maybe ninety percent.

The rest of him

looks like a fancy dog."

20

"If he is part mutt,

he is all mutt," said Grandfather.

Marisol parted his fur.

"Uh-oh!" she said.

"Now I see a couple of fleas.

We better get him a flea collar."

"*¡Qué cosa!*" said Grandfather.

"Whoever heard of putting

a flea collar on a stray dog?"

"Oh, Grandpa, please let me buy one

with the money Uncle Cuco gave me

for my birthday."

Grandfather shrugged.

"I suppose you can buy what you wish

with your own money," he said,

"but don't think

this dog is going to like

having a collar around his neck."

At Doña Elvira's store,

there were flea collars in two sizes:

medium and large.

"Is he a medium dog or a large dog?"

asked Doña Elvira.

"He is sort of medium large,"
said Marisol.

"I think he is more medium
than large," said Grandfather.

Marisol nodded.

"I think so, too," she said.

When they got back to the house,

the dog sat very still while Marisol

put the flea collar on him.

"That's odd," said Grandfather.

"I didn't think he would like it."

"He loves it," said Marisol proudly.

At bedtime, Marisol said,

"The dog is in the yard, *Abuelito*.

Is it okay if he sleeps there?"

"I don't see any way to stop him,"

said Grandfather.

"There is a full moon,

so he will not be in the dark,"

said Marisol. "And when it rains,

he can keep dry

under the mango tree."

"Uh-huh," said Grandfather.

"Grandpa! He's asleep!" said Marisol.

"I guess he feels at home,"

said Grandfather.

Marisol's eyes brightened. "At home?"

"I didn't say this *was* his home.

I just said he *feels* at home.

Now go to bed," said Grandfather.

"Grandpa!" Marisol called,
"you forgot to kiss me good night."
Marisol heard the floor creak,
as Grandfather got up
and crossed the room
in his bare feet.

"Sleep well, Mari," he said.

Marisol smiled. "That is what I said
when I said good night to Pancho."

"Pancho?" said Grandfather.

"Who is Pancho?"

"My dog," said Marisol.

"I named him Pancho."

The Search

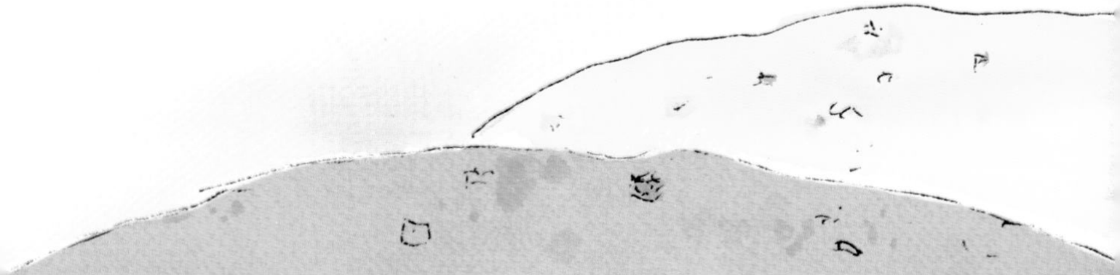

At supper the next day,

they had stew.

There were no leftovers.

Marisol did not say anything,

but Grandfather could see

she was unhappy.

"Give him a little chopped meat

from the refrigerator," he said.

"Does chopped meat cost a lot?"

asked Marisol.

"It costs plenty," said Grandfather.

34

"Maybe we should get him
some dry dog food," said Marisol.
"I certainly cannot afford
to feed him chopped meat,"
said Grandfather.

When they returned from the *colmado*

later that evening,

Grandfather carried the groceries.

Marisol carried a bag of dog food.

But Pancho was not there.

He was not there

when Marisol woke up

the next morning,

nor the morning after that.

"Don't worry," said Grandfather.

"If anything happened to Pancho,

Nando or Doña Elvira would tell us."

Marisol ran to talk to Nando
before he went fishing.

"Nando, have you seen Pancho?"

asked Marisol.

"He hasn't been home

for two days and two nights."

"Hmm," said Nando.

"He has probably found

a female dog that he likes."

"You mean Pancho has a girlfriend?"

asked Marisol.

"Why not? He is a healthy young dog.

Come fishing with me, Mari.

The snappers are biting real good.

It will take your mind off the dog."

"No, thanks, Nando," said Marisol.

"I want to speak to Doña Elvira."

Inside the *colmado*

it was cool and dark.

"Doña Elvira, have you seen my dog?"

asked Marisol.

"He disappeared two days ago."

"No," said Doña Elvira.

"I have not seen him,

and I *always* notice Pancho."

43

"Pancho may have a female friend,"
said Doña Elvira.

"That's what Nando thinks,"
said Marisol.

Doña Elvira gave Marisol
a lemon drop and a lollypop.

"Take these," she said,

"and don't worry about Pancho."

Marisol woke up

in the middle of the night.

She felt her way to the door

and called Pancho's name.

Pancho was not in the yard.

As she walked back to her room,
she bumped into Grandfather.

"Marisol, what are you doing up
in the middle of the night?"

"I was looking for Pancho.

What were *you* doing?"

asked Marisol.

"I was looking for him, too."

Grandfather led her back to bed
and tucked her in.

"I don't know why I love
such a foolish little girl,"
he said.

Marisol looked at him shyly.

"I don't know why I love

such a foolish old grandpa."

Pancho Saves the Day

"Wake up, Marisol. He's back!

Pancho is back!" said Grandfather.

Marisol jumped out of bed

and ran outdoors.

"Pancho!" she cried.

She hugged him again and again.

Grandfather brought out

a big bowl of dog food.

Doña Elvira came running.

"*¡Lo vi!*" she shouted. "I saw him!
I saw Pancho."

Just then, Nando came up the hill
with two red snappers.
"Pancho is home!"
Marisol called out.

"Where have you been, Pancho?"

Nando asked.

He knelt down and put his ear

up to the dog's nose.

Nando nodded to the dog

and then stood up.

"It is just as I thought," he said.

"Pancho has a girlfriend."

"What did I tell you,"

said Doña Elvira. "Look at him.

Skinny, chewed up, and worn out."

Marisol kneeled down
and put her ear to the dog's nose,
the way Nando had.
"Are you sure he said that, Nando?
I can't hear anything."

"Nobody can, except Nando,"
said Grandfather.

"That's true," said Doña Elvira.

"Nando is the only one on the hill
who understands dog talk."

That evening,

when Marisol and Grandfather

sat down to dinner,

they heard Pancho barking.

Grandfather got up

to see what was the matter.

There was a pot of rice

burning on the stove.

Pancho was barking

because of the smoke.

"Thanks, Pancho," Grandfather said

and turned off the stove.

"What happened?" asked Marisol.

"Why did you say, 'Thanks, Pancho'?"

"Because," said Grandfather,

"he smelled something burning

and warned us."

"Oh, Grandpa," said Marisol,
"aren't we lucky to have Pancho?
What if he had not been here?"
"We could have had a fire,"
said Grandfather.

At bedtime Marisol was quiet.

"*¿Qué pasa?*" asked Grandfather.

"What's the matter?"

"Nothing. I just wondered
if Pancho really is our dog."

"Marisol," said Grandfather,

"I told you from the start
that once you feed a dog,
he thinks you own him."

"Do we own him?" asked Marisol.

Grandfather chuckled.

"I don't know," he said.

"But he sure owns us."

"Does that mean

we will always feed him?"

"I guess so," said Grandfather.

"He is a good watchdog."

Marisol hugged Grandfather.

"I love you, *Abuelito*," said Marisol.

"I love you, too, Mari.

But remember,

Pancho is an outside dog.

And he will always be

an outside dog."

"Of course," said Marisol.
"I have always wanted
an outside dog."